Bubbie and Zadie Come to My House

A STORY FOR HANUKKAH

Daniel Halevi Bloom

Illustrations by Alex Meilichson

COVER DESIGNER: Jeannie Tudor
TYPESETTER: Jeannie Tudor

Square One Publishers
115 Herricks Road
Garden City Park, NY 11040
(516) 535-2010 • (877) 900-BOOK
www.SquareOnePublishers.com

Library of Congress Cataloging-in-Publication Data

Bloom, Daniel Halevi.
Bubbie and Zadie come to my house : a story for Hanukkah /
Daniel Halevi Bloom; illustrations by Alex Meilichson.
p. cm.
Summary: Bubbie and Zadie, two magical characters, bring the spirit of Hanukkah to a Jewish family on the first night of the holiday.
ISBN 0-7570-0298-6 (hardcover)
[1. Hanukkah—Fiction.] I. Meilichson, Alex, ill. II. Title.
PZ7.B6228Bu 2006
[E]—dc22

200601751

Printed in the United States of America

10 9 8 7 6 5 4 3 2 1

This book is dedicated to the children of this world
who have not yet lost the power to believe
in things beyond ordinary understanding.
And to all **Bubbies** and **Zadies** the world over,
no matter what their faith or philosophy.
And to my parents, who gave me
the most precious gift of all— life!
Go, little book, and find your world.

FOR AS LONG as I can remember, Hanukkah was different from the other holidays. Potato latkes would be cooking on the griddle . . . Mother had Hanukkah cookies baking in the oven, too. Outside, in the cold December air, snow would be falling from the night sky, creating a fairyland of shapes on the bushes and trees around our house.

It was Hanukkah, but it was Christmastime, too. Some of our neighbors' houses were brightly lit with colored lights, and decorated trees stood in their living room windows. Inside our house, a beautiful menorah shone just as brightly as any Christmas tree on the block!

What made Hanukkah extra special ever since I can remember is that Bubbie and Zadie would come to visit! Yes, Bubbie and Zadie, whose names mean "grandma" and "grandpa" in the Hebrew language, are two magical friends who always reminded me of my very own grandparents.

Like my grandparents, this Bubbie and Zadie are wise and full of advice. They love to tell stories as much as they love to hear them, especially the story of Hanukkah. And they love children, especially *you*! That is why, on the first night of Hanukkah, they visit Jewish children all over the world. They are able to do this through their magical powers. This is what happens . . .

As soon as the sun goes down, they stand on the doorstep of their little house, which is located in a tiny village in Alaska. Beneath a sky filled with a million and one stars, and with the Northern Lights glowing above them, they hold hands, close their eyes, and say,

"Shalom aleichem shalom! Shalom aleichem shalom! Shalom aleichem shalom!"

(In the Hebrew language, *shalom aleichem* means "peace be with you.")

And then, through a mysterious power, Bubbie and Zadie fly through the air, as if they are lifted by the memories of all the bubbies and zadies that have come before them. And as they travel, they bring with them the spirit of Hanukkah itself.

Do you know what the spirit of Hanukkah is?

It is a little girl listening to her grandmother tell stories of a time when she herself celebrated Hanukkah as a little girl.

It is a little boy sitting next to his grandfather and spinning the dreidel, watching to see which letters will turn up—*nun, gimmel, hay or shin*. Altogether, these letters mean "A great miracle happened there." And what is the great miracle of Hanukkah? It is a story of old.

The spirit of Hanukkah is also families gathering together to celebrate the special meaning of the Festival of Lights.

The spirit of Hanukkah is life itself. It is . . . *L'chayim*!

What a wonderful celebration we have on this special holiday!

The very first time Bubbie and Zadie came to my house, I was seven years old. It was the first night of Hanukkah. My sister and I were in the living room, where we had just helped our parents light the menorah. We were staring at the colored candles as the flames lit up the room and made pretty shadows on the wall. Our parents were in the kitchen, visiting with friends who had come by.
We always had many guests on that night. Maybe you do, too!

Suddenly, there was a gentle knocking on the door. Thump! Thump! Only my sister and I seemed to hear it.

I went to the door and opened it ever so slightly.

There stood a little man and woman, all bundled up against the cold.

"Who are you?" I asked.

"I'm Bubbie," the woman said, and she looked a lot like my grandmother.

"And I'm Zadie," said the little man, and he reminded me of my grandfather!

Were they really my grandparents? Or was this just a dream? Before I could make up my mind, Bubbie said, "Thank you for opening the door for us on this first night of Hanukkah. We have come a long way to visit you."

Somehow, my sister and I knew that Bubbie and Zadie were very special people.

Bubbie and Zadie slowly floated through the doorway into our house. That's right. They didn't walk through the door like regular people. They floated. You must remember that Bubbie and Zadie are not regular people—they are magical. They are also much too magical to see with your eyes. But if you try, you *can* see them if you use the eyes inside your mind—your imagination. Everyone has an imagination. In this book, you will see what Bubbie and Zadie looked like to me!

"Shalom aleichem," my sister said. "Welcome to our home!" They replied, *"Aleichem shalom."*

Zadie shook the stardust from his boots and said, "You are very special children because you believe in us. We have come here tonight to bring you good luck and to remind you of something very valuable—the importance of a good heart! A good heart is like a pretty candle burning in the menorah. It can light up the world. This is something you must remember always."

My grandfather had told me the same thing, and now Zadie reminded me of him all the more.

"Are you hungry?" I asked. "Would you like some fruit?"

"Why, yes," they both said.

So I went into the kitchen and returned with a bowl that was filled with apples, pears, bananas, and some grapes. Bubbie, Zadie, and my sister were sitting at the table, looking through a book of Hanukkah stories. I joined them.

“Do you know why we light the Hanukkah candles?” Zadie asked after taking a bite of a pear.

“Oh yes, the story of Hanukkah is very old, and we tell it every year,” my sister said.

Remembering the lessons our parents had taught us, I said, “It is to remember the miracle of the oil, which happened in the Temple of Jerusalem long, long ago. The Maccabees had been fighting for their religion. Their enemies, the ancient Assyrian-Greeks, wanted to kill them and stop the Jewish religion. But the Maccabees fought back and the Jewish people survived.”

“To celebrate their victory,” my sister said, “the Maccabees wanted to dedicate the Temple to God once again. But they had only enough oil in their lamps to burn for one day. Somehow, the oil burned for eight whole days! It was a miracle!”

Bubbie and Zadie looked at both of us proudly. They were pleased that we knew the story of the ancient Maccabees and the miracle of the burning oil.

Zadie said, “The Maccabees were once again able to pray in their Temple. For the Jewish people, this was and still is very important.” Then he told us something we did not know. He told us that the word “Hanukkah” means “dedication” in the Hebrew language.

All this time, our parents and the other grownups didn't seem to hear us talking. I don't think they even knew that Bubbie and Zadie were in our house!

"Come, let's spin the dreidel," Zadie suddenly said.

My sister and I were happy to play the dreidel game. It was always fun to watch the spinning dreidel slow down and drop onto its side. The letter that appeared on top would tell us if we could take some walnuts from the bowl on the table.

As the dreidel twirled, Bubbie and Zadie began to quietly sing:

Dreidel, dreidel, dreidel
I made you out of clay
And when you're dry and ready,
Oh dreidel I will play.

My sister and I knew that Hanukkah song, too! So with the next spin, we sang along with Bubbie and Zadie:

It has a lovely body
With legs so short and thin
And when it gets all tired
It drops and then I win!

When it was my turn, I spun the dreidel and it stopped on *hay*. Zadie clapped his hands in delight as Bubbie put walnuts in my lap.

"What's going on in there?" my mother called from the kitchen.

"We're just playing dreidel and singing," I answered.

My sister and I laughed, and Bubbie and Zadie laughed, too, as we continued spinning the dreidel and singing the Hanukkah song.

Now I must confess that I had been curious about something from the moment Bubbie and Zadie first knocked on our door. I wondered how they were able to travel to our house and to so many others on this first night of Hanukkah. Did they drive a car? Did they take a bus or a plane? Maybe you were wondering this, too.

I ran to the window and looked outside, but there was no sign of how our two magical visitors had come to our house. I turned to them and finally asked, "Bubbie and Zadie, how did you get here?"

As they stood there in the middle of the room, Bubbie and Zadie turned to each other and smiled broadly. Then they joined hands and said, "*Shalom aleichem shalom*" three times. Before I could blink my eyes, they were flying in the air! Up, up, up they went. They soared over the table, over the bowl of walnuts, over the cuckoo clock, and over the sofa. They flew around the room like birds. They flew this way and that, up and down. They flew sideways and upside down. They flew backwards and forwards. My sister and I couldn't believe our eyes!

Then just as suddenly, Bubbie and Zadie landed back on the floor without a sound. Bubbie gave us a big hug, then Zadie gave us one, too. It was a feeling I would always remember.

Suddenly, I noticed the candles on the menorah were getting shorter. I knew what that meant. Even my watch told me it was getting later and later. Soon it would be bedtime.

All at once, Bubbie reached for her coat. She said, "I'm afraid the time has come for us to leave. We have many more children to visit tonight."

"Will you come back
next year?" I asked.

As he put on his hat
Zadie smiled and whispered,
"Dear children, once you
have opened your hearts to us,
we will always come back.
Always . . ."

As Bubbie buttoned up her coat,
she said, "Remember, you can write to
us whenever you wish. We are always
happy to hear from our friends."

My sister and I did not want to say
goodbye, but we knew that Bubbie
and Zadie had to leave. We gave
them each a final hug.

Suddenly we felt a cool breeze in the room. The Hanukkah candles flickered this way and that on the windowsill. I looked out the window and could see the stars twinkling far, far away.

When I turned back to Bubbie and Zadie, they were gone! Just like that! As magically as they had appeared, they disappeared into the night sky!

My sister and I ran to the window. As the candles flickered one last time before going out, we were sure we could see our two magical friends floating above the rooftops. And even though they were high in the sky, we could hear them say, "*Shalom aleichem,* dear children! Happy Hanukkah!"

When I knew that Bubbie and Zadie were really gone, at first I felt sad inside. Whenever you love someone very much, it always makes you sad to see them go, but the joy you have shared will always be in your heart.

Even now as a grownup, the memory of my Bubbie and Zadie stays with me. Every Hanukkah, I smile when I think of them and the lessons they taught my sister and me.

Bubbie and Zadie love getting mail from children.
If you would like to handwrite a letter
to them, you can mail it to:

BUBBIE AND ZADIE'S MAILBOX
c/o Square One Publishers
115 Herricks Road
Garden City Park, NY 11040

If you would like to write an e-mail letter to
Bubbie and Zadie, you can send it to:

bubbie.zadie@gmail.com

You can even write to them if you are a
grownup. Many grownups do!

About the Author

Daniel Halevi Bloom grew up in Springfield, Massachusetts, in a family of five children, and graduated from Tufts University with an honors degree in literature. The author of seven children's books, including *In the Eyes of a Child, It's Never Too Late to Begin Again* and *Tasty, Tantalizing, Terrific: Taiwan,* Mr. Bloom has worked over the years as a cartoonist, a newspaper editor, a public relations consultant, and a freelance journalist. He has lived for extended periods of time in Europe, Alaska, Japan, and Taiwan. You can learn more about Mr. Bloom and his works by visiting his website at *http://bubbieandzadie.blogspot.com*.

About the Illustrator

Alex Meilichson was born in Venezuela, but later emigrated to Israel with his family. There, he studied sociology and political science at Tel Aviv University. He has also studied art and art history at the University of Berlin; in Caracas, Venezuela; and at the Art Students League in New York.

Acknowledgments

A special Internet thanks to Susan Anderson in Virginia, Karen Waldrip in Alaska, Manny Kopstein in California, and Roberta Flude in Australia. Thanks also to the many angels out there in Readerland who have written to Bubbie and Zadie over the past years. And finally, thanks to all of the bubbies and zadies now residing at Bubbie and Zadie's House (*www.bubbie-zadieshouse.com*) in San Rafael, California.